The Case of the

Grave Accusation

The Case of the Grave Accusation

A Sherlock Holmes Adventure

As Recited from the Papers and
the Personal Narrative of
Dr. John H. Watson

Written by
Dicky Neely

Edited by
Paul R. Spiring

MX Publishing

Paperback: ISBN 9781908218810
Mobipocket/Kindle: ISBN 9781908218827
ePub/iBook: ISBN 9781908218834

Published in the UK by MX Publishing Limited,
335 Princess Park Manor, Royal Drive,
London, N11 3GX.
www.mxpublishing.com

Cover design by Staunch Design,
11 Shipton Road,
Woodstock,
Oxfordshire, OX20 1LW.
www.staunch.com

About the Contributors

Dicky Neely (Author and Illustrator) was born in 1947 in Marshall, a small town nestled in the pine woods of North East Texas. He has written many articles for windsurfing magazines and has also drawn cartoons for numerous other publications. After moving to Corpus Christi on the Texas Gulf Coast, Neely started writing for local newspapers. He still writes for *We the People* and maintains a number of weblogs. Neely has enjoyed reading all his life and is particularly fond of the Sherlock Holmes stories. His other passion is for blues music, and he attributes this to the sound of lonesome train whistles, which he heard as a boy. Neely has sung and played harmonica in many blues bands over the years.

Paul R. Spiring (Editor) is both a chartered biologist and physicist. He is currently seconded by the U.K. Government to work as a biology teacher within the English section of the European School of Karlsruhe in Germany. Paul is the joint author of three books: *On the Trail of Arthur Conan Doyle, A Footnote to The Hound of the Baskervilles* and *Arthur Conan Doyle, Sherlock Holmes and Devon* and he has compiled five other books. Paul also maintains a tribute website that commemorates the memory of Bertram Fletcher Robinson (http://www.bfronline.biz) and is a member of The Sherlock Holmes Society of London, La Société Sherlock Holmes de France, The Conan Doyle (Crowborough) Establishment, The Crew of the S.S. May Day and The Sydney Passengers.

Frontispiece. The Hound of the Baskervilles.

The Hound of the Baskervilles by Arthur Conan Doyle was first serialised as nine monthly episodes within the British edition of *The Strand Magazine* (August 1901 – April 1902). This plate by Sidney Paget accompanied the first instalment of the story in that same periodical (Vol. XXII, No. 128, p. 122). It depicts the 'coal-black' spectral 'hell-hound' in hot pursuit of the 'wicked Hugo Baskerville' across Dartmoor in Devon.

To my sister Jan

She has always encouraged me

xxx

Contents

Preface

When I was growing-up I became a compulsive reader. Around the age of eleven or so, I started reading many of the Victorian and Edwardian writers, including Sir Arthur Conan Doyle. I particularly loved his Sherlock Holmes stories. I have read and re-read the Holmes canon many times and I have also enjoyed the many cinema and TV dramatisations, especially the Granada TV adaptation of *The Return of Sherlock Holmes* starring Jeremy Brett.

Around the turn of this century, I read that a man in England had claimed that Conan Doyle stole the story of *The Hound of the Baskervilles* from a friend called Bertram Fletcher Robinson. As if that was not bad enough, it was also claimed that Conan Doyle then convinced the man's wife to poison him with laudanum in order to conceal the act of plagiarism. Knowing full well that Conan Doyle had fully acknowledged Fletcher Robinson's help in a footnote to the first serialised edition of *The Hound of the Baskervilles*, I felt that these allegations were bunkum, and decided to explore the matter further.

The result was my Holmes pastiche *The Case of the Grave Accusation*, in which I transport the Baker Street detective and his sidekick into the future to investigate the case. This story was first published during 2002 in a now defunct Texan newspaper entitled the *Coastal Bend Sun* and I was paid $150.00 for which I was grateful.

Dicky Neely
June 2011
Corpus Christi

Chapter I

Do not fail me now!

I have experienced many strange and wondrous things during my long association with Mr. Sherlock Holmes. Throughout all our adventures, Holmes never sought riches for himself, and he remained content to live a modest existence at our flat at 221B Baker Street in London. For Holmes the mere satisfaction of solving a mystery and of succeeding where others had failed was sufficient reward in itself.

Initially, I flattered myself that I was an aid to Holmes in the application of his methods but I soon realised that I was merely his foil. In fact, Holmes even mocked that *my* obtuseness was *his* most effective tool in the fight against crime!

One of my passions was for writing reminiscences of our adventures. Many of these were serialised in *The*

Strand Magazine and they helped to gain Holmes a legion of admirers. However, he disdained adulation and therefore attached little import to my literary work.

It has now been many years since we ranged the foggy streets of London in pursuit of malefactors and time has had its inevitable effect on us both. But we are, after all, fictional characters, and as such we have a bit more latitude than real people and sometimes amazing things may be wrought upon the pages of fiction.

That brings me to the question of why I am addressing you now. Well, I had resigned myself to spend eternity in the limbo of literary characters whose lives exist only on the pages of books that were written long ago. So, imagine my great surprise when I received the following handwritten note:

Watson, come to Baker Street as soon as possible. It is most urgent. Do not fail me now! Sherlock Holmes.

This electrified me! Without a second thought, I shook off the dust of the ages and hotfooted my way to Charing Cross tube station. I was somewhat perturbed by the strange paraphernalia that I saw about me and by the odd way that my fellow passengers were dressed. For their part, few noticed me, and none conversed with me directly. Evidently, whilst my attire was to put it mildly, a little antiquated, the London Underground is a place where idiosyncratic fashion is commonplace and therefore goes largely unnoticed.

The underground train conveyed me with incredible velocity to my egress point and I was soon standing on Baker Street again. Though the old Hansom cabs had been replaced by machines that I immediately deduced to be automobiles, my old neighbourhood was much the same as I remembered.

I confess that my heart was pounding as I sounded the doorbell to 221B. To my great surprise, I was greeted by Wiggins, one of the many Baker Street irregulars, who let me in and then escorted me to my rooms. On entering, I was choked by an acrid plume of tobacco smoke that drifted towards me from the direction of the study-desk.

"Watson! Come in, come in!" shouted Holmes. "I am so glad that you are here at long last!"

"I can't believe my eyes! Holmes, it is so good to see you again my dear friend!"

Holmes bolted at me from behind the desk, shook my hand, and gave me a quick pat on the right shoulder.

"Watson! Sit down and I shall fill you in on the facts as I know them to be. This is surely the most insidious case that has ever confronted us!"

At that moment the door swung open and Mrs. Hudson entered the room with her best silver serving tray and bone china tea service. She welcomed me with a sober smile and then started to pour two cups of tea. I moved towards her with a view to shaking her by the hand. However, she promptly flushed scarlet and escaped to the door. "Well, I must let the two of you get down to work!" she said before rapidly retreating.

Holmes chuckled to himself as he reached into his Persian slipper for yet more tobacco. It was business as usual!

Chapter II

Down to business

Holmes ended the reverie abruptly with the perfunctory words, "Well! Now down to business. Ah, the joy of a worthy challenge! It's like old times Watson."

I could sense that he was enervated by the prospect of engaging his deductive powers again. Holmes strode to the bookshelf, picked out a folder, and handed it to me.

"Herein Watson, you will find printed materials that are pertinent to our case. I have gathered them from various newspapers and other sources."

Tell me what necessitates our revival!" I demanded.

"Our reputations and very existence are threatened" said Holmes as he paced back and forth. He added, "This is a remarkable age Watson. They have marvels we could scarcely imagine! What I would have given to have had available to me some of the tools that are commonplace in this time!" Holmes appeared to be unsure of where to go next before he finally continued thus:

"To make a long story short we must fight to protect the reputation of our creator, and Literary Agent, Sir Arthur Conan Doyle. He stands accused of plagiarism!"

"Plagiarism!" I stammered in disbelief. "Who has made this allegation?"

Holmes frowned as he continued, "I need not explain to you the gravity of the situation. If the charge is proven to be true, or even perceived to be so, we will lose all credibility and be destroyed!"

"Please reveal all!" said I.

"Naturally." said Holmes. "Do you recall a man by the name of Bertram Fletcher Robinson?"

"Fletcher Robinson! Why yes. He was an acquaintance of Sir Arthur and a writer. I also remember that he died shortly before Sir Arthur remarried in 1907." I replied.

Holmes nodded before adding, "Do you also recall that Conan Doyle planned to visit his home in Devon prior to the publication of *The Hound of the Baskervilles*? "

"So?" I responded.

"It is claimed that during this visit, Fletcher Robinson disclosed to his guest some unpublished tale that he had written about Dartmoor and then introduced him to a servant named Henry Baskerville. Do you see where all this is going Watson?"

"Good God Holmes! This sounds very serious! So the plagiarism charge may be true?" I could scarcely credit what I was hearing.

"It does look bad on the face of it. However, we must investigate further before formulating any conclusions!" proclaimed Holmes as he strode across the room to a window that overlooked Baker Street.

"The plot thickens as they say. There is more, much more, and it is repugnant in nature!" said Holmes in a hushed voice.

"What could be worse than this?" I choked.

"Murder most foul! At least that is what Conan Doyle's accuser would have us believe." said Holmes solemnly.

"Murder!" I repeated incredulously.

"A modern day author called Roger la Pelure d'Ail has just published a catalogue of charges. He claims that after stealing the idea for *The Hound of the Baskervilles*, Conan Doyle committed adultery with Mrs. Fletcher Robinson, and then blackmailed her into poisoning her husband with laudanum so as to conceal the act of plagiarism. He also makes much of the fact that Conan Doyle was a physician and therefore knew that this drug would elude casual detection." said Holmes.

"But, this is preposterous! What evidence is there?" I

9

remonstrated.

"Watson, it seems that in some ways this age is much like our own. It is relatively easy to make a serious charge but very difficult to disprove it. More often than not a false accusation is perceived to be true and it sticks. We should be receiving a visitor soon who may cast more light upon this matter. Indeed, I believe that he is arriving as we speak." said Holmes as he peered through the window into the street below.

I joined Holmes by the window and glanced across the road to a dark automobile that had pulled-up beside the curb. The door of the vehicle swung open and a ferret-like man in his forties stepped-out onto the pavement. I speculated to myself that even in this new era, I could still distinguish between a member of the constabulary and the general public.

Chapter III

Moore of 'The Yard'

I listened attentively to the footsteps which climbed the seventeen stairs that ascend to our rooms. Eventually, they halted and Mrs. Hudson opened the door and duly announced, "There's a gentleman here to see you Mr. Holmes."

"Show him in Mrs. Hudson!" urged Holmes with an airiness of manner that was atypical.

The lean man that I had seen moments before alighting from his automobile now entered our room. He had a rat-like face, dark eyes and a thick head of auburn hair. He wore a dark-grey suit, blue shirt and red tie, and was carrying a brown attaché case in his left hand. For my part, it was difficult not to stare because I was still unaccustomed to the modern fashion. Holmes seemed nonplused and carried on as if he had been born in the Twenty-First Century.

The man shook our hands firmly. "It's really a pleasure to meet you both. We have quite a file about you at New Scotland Yard and our Information Technology system is called Holmes 2 in your honour! Why it is partly down to you that The Yard now enjoys such an excellent reputation! My name is Detective Inspector Andrew Moore and I am at your service."

"You must understand Mr. Moore that my colleague Dr. Watson and I are in an unusual situation and therefore we must observe the utmost caution. Do you have some credentials?"

"Yes of course!" said Moore appearing somewhat crestfallen. He set down his attaché case and reached into his jacket pocket to produce a rather worn wallet. He then flipped it open to display a warrant card, which was tucked away behind a heap of plastic cards, and several colour photographs. Holmes then turned his back on us and took two steps towards the desk before enquiring politely:

"Mr. Moore, are your two daughters doing well at the catholic school? It must be hard to balance the demands of your career with those of being a single parent!"

"How do you know all this Mr. Holmes? I heard you were sharp but this...?" Moore was the personification of astonishment.

I too was surprised but knowing Holmes' methods, I kept my silence, realising full well that all would soon be revealed.

Holmes smiled before he replied, "It is most elementary Mr. Moore! You do not wear a wedding ring and yet you carry pictures of two young girls with resplendent auburn hair with you at all times. Hence, I wager that they are your daughters, and that you are estranged from the mother. In the inside pocket of your jacket you also carry a program for a musical production that was recently performed at the Sisters of Mercy School in South Norwood. These facts suggest a lone father whose primary concern is for the moral welfare of his children. Furthermore, your wardrobe suggests a frugality that is in keeping with a man that places the contentment of his daughters ahead of his own. Really, it is nothing difficult to understand!"

The colour rose in Moore's cheeks. After a short and uncomfortable interval he broke into a broad grin and laughed aloud, "Mr. Holmes, I can see your reputation is well deserved sir!"

Holmes continued, "Mr. Moore let us get down to the task at hand. I assume that you know why we are here? Please tell us all you know."

Moore nodded before he responded, "Gentlemen it is of course a most unusual case. The basics are this. As you know one Mr. Roger la Pelure d'Ail has just published a book about the relationship between Sir Arthur Conan Doyle and a contemporary called Mr. Bertram Fletcher Robinson. He alleges that Conan Doyle appropriated the tale of *The Hound of the Baskervilles* from Fletcher Robinson and then committed adultery with his wife in order to…" Holmes interrupted impatiently, "I know all this! What else is there?"

"…well, la Pelure d'Ail wants us to exhume Fletcher Robinson's body and to test whether he died from poisoning, or from typhoid, which is the official cause of his death." added Moore guardedly.

"I see! Watson, I think that you and I should travel to Dartmoor again. Mr. Moore, please keep us abreast of any developments at this end. I will let you know where we can be reached." said Holmes as he rose from his chair and beckoned our visitor towards the door.

"Here is my card Mr. Holmes. It lists my telephone numbers, fax number and email addresses. Good bye then gentleman, and I trust that we shall meet again very soon." said Moore before taking his leave of us.

"Fax number? Email addresses? What on earth is he talking about Holmes?" Clearly, I still had much to learn!

Chapter IV

The Baker Street posse

After Detective Inspector Moore had departed, Holmes fell silent for several minutes. Then, without facing me, he suddenly asked, "Watson, did our visitor remind you of anyone?"

"No. Did he remind you of somebody then?" I replied.

"Perhaps..." said Holmes with a quizzical expression on his aquiline face.

"I have it!" he exclaimed. "Detective Inspector Moore bears a striking resemblance to our old friend Inspector Lestrade! I must make discreet enquiries to see whether there is some family connection."

"Lestrade! Why yes, I believe that you may be right."

Holmes strode quickly to a closed cabinet on the wall behind the desk. "Look here Watson. I have been making an attempt to get in step with the modern age."

He opened the cabinet to reveal a strange box-like contraption that was attached to a bewildering array of wires. It was attached by yet another wire to a smaller rectangular object which was covered in buttons.

"This Watson is a desktop computer and what a truly marvellous invention it is! If only we had had access to such a machine in our day!"

"A computer you say? What does it do?" I was baffled.

"A computer is an electronic machine that reveals facts at the press of a button. With this device all is revealed! This is the keyboard and this object is called a mouse."

"Mouse? Balderdash! It looks like no mouse that I ever saw!" I snorted.

Holmes ignored my protests and continued, "Wiggins recruited a new group of irregulars upon my return.

These juveniles refer to themselves as the Baker Street posse and they know all there is to know about computers. Some of them have been instructing me in its operation. Look!"

Holmes made a swift movement with his right hand and a picture appeared upon the screen. Several more clicks later and the screen swirled into a blur of activity that was unintelligible to me. Finally, the screen settled on an image of Detective Inspector Andrew Moore beside a silver sign that read New Scotland Yard. The picture was impressive enough but it was accompanied by his entire biography! Here it was written that Moore had indeed descended from a family which had a long association with The Yard. The text also listed some of the major cases that he had helped to solve during his twenty-two years of police service. I was agog!

"This is a remarkable device. However we might have deduced its invention given the steady advancement of science and technology during our time." said Holmes.

He then handed me a thick leather-bound book. "This is a rare first edition of *The Complete Sherlock Holmes.* Turn to the start of *The Hound of the Baskervilles.*

I consulted the index and eagerly thumbed my way to the relevant page.

"Read the footnote!" ordered Holmes.

I placed my reading glasses in position and read the following acknowledgement aloud:

"My Dear Fletcher Robinson. It was your account of a west country legend which first suggested the idea of this little tale to my mind. For this, and for the help you gave me in its evolution, all thanks. Yours, most truly, A. Conan Doyle."

"What do you make of it?" enquired Holmes.

"I say that it refutes the charge of plagiarism!"

"Agreed but we must not leap to any conclusion before we have ascertained all the facts Watson."

"What should be our first course of action?" I asked.

"We must travel to Dartmoor to see what else can be learned there. I suggest that we visit Fox Tor Mires, Princetown and Fletcher Robinson's former home at Ipplepen."

"That is a capitol idea Holmes and the country air will also do us good."

"Well then Watson, let us grab a quick bite to eat, and retire to bed early. Tomorrow we have much to do!"

Mrs. Hudson served us a meal of Cornish hen, russet potatoes and corn. We washed it down with a bottle of Cabernet Sauvignon from the vintage 1999! Clearly, Mrs. Hudson was enjoying her respite from literary limbo as much as we.

After dinner, I retired upstairs to my bedroom, and was serenaded to sleep by the faint strains of Holmes' violin.

Chapter V

The game is afoot

Next morning, I awoke to Holmes tugging away at my elbow. "It's time to wake Watson! The game is afoot." Once he was satisfied that I was reanimating he added, "Mrs. Hudson will have breakfast prepared in fifteen minutes." He then left me to myself and I reluctantly stepped-out of bed.

No sooner had I begun to dress then Holmes returned. "Pardon my intrusion but I have taken the liberty of purchasing for you some attire that is more in keeping with the contemporary fashion." He placed the clothing on my bed and bolted before I could voice any protest.

I took the shirt and put it on. I was impressed by the fabric which was cotton according to a label affixed to the collar. The trousers too were both lightweight and comfortable. Holmes had also provided a pair of shoes and stockings and, after donning these, I trudged into the dining room and joined him at the table.

Breakfast was a tumultuous affair! We had French wheat cakes with honey and homemade butter followed by poached eggs and sweet cured ham. Mrs. Hudson also plied us with Turkish coffee that was both strong and aromatic. Holmes and I spoke little as we savoured our regal repast!

After breakfast we retreated to the drawing room for a pipe. Thereafter, Holmes produced a brown Gladstone bag that was stuffed to capacity with assorted papers. These items included a map of Dartmoor, numerous newspaper articles, and several printed pages which related to a hotel reservation. It transpired that Holmes had produced many of the pages himself using a device called a laser printer!

"Watson, we depart for Devonshire today. I have hired a private automobile and the driver should be arriving here in a few moments. I think that our trip will be most illuminating."

I replied warily, "I once drove a little Ford and I did not

care for it much! It was a noisy contraption and rather dangerous too as I seem to recall!"

"I believe that modern vehicles can still be dangerous. However, you can now judge the matter for yourself. I observe that our automobile and driver have just drawn-up outside." said Holmes.

I leaned over and peered nervously through the window at a black automobile parked opposite. Beyond the fact that it is now referred to as a car, I was ignorant of what I beheld. Nevertheless the sleek metal machine was an impressive sight to these old eyes! The offside door opened and the driver climbed out and knocked on the door to 221B. A few moments later Mrs. Hudson materialised and she announced, "Gentlemen, this is Mr. Covington your driver."

"Thank you Mrs. Hudson. Do come in Covington. My name is Sherlock Holmes and this is my colleague, Dr. Watson."

Holmes beckoned to the man to come forward and we took it in turns to shake his hand. "Pleased to meet you gents…tis a rare honour sirs" said Covington. He was about fifty and was wearing a dark grey suit and tie.

"We are ready Covington. Our bags are downstairs and we are both looking forward to a pleasant drive in the country." said Holmes.

"I can assure you of that sir. Well let's be off then." With that we descended the stairway and Covington deposited our luggage in a storage space at the rear of the car. Before departing, Holmes gave Covington two pages of printed material, which outlined the itinerary for our trip. He read it over and said, "Very good sir! I know Devon well. I grew up there. It's a lovely place!"

We motored from Baker Street to Oxford Street and from there to Regent Street. I was impressed with how smooth and rapid the car was in its operation. We then passed along Pall Mall, Saint James's Street, Picadilly, Hyde Park Road and Knightsbridge before joining a multi-lane highway called the M4 motorway.

Covington proved to be a skilful driver. He seemed perfectly at ease driving at high speed amidst an array of other vehicles. He also merged most assuredly with heavy traffic at a bewildering intersection between the M4 and M5 motorways near the city of Bristol.

Chapter VI

The return to Dartmoor

Throughout the duration of our journey Holmes said nothing. Instead he kept his rapt gaze fixed upon the vista unfolding outside. It was apparent to me that he was deeply immersed in thought and so I left him be.

After Bristol we turned south towards Princetown, which was our final destination. Within the hour we had reached the A38 Devon Expressway that connects Exeter and Plymouth. Little had changed since my first visit to the area over a century ago. Indeed it appeared that the very same 'Red Ruby' cows were grazing on the lush vegetation that issued forth from the rust coloured soil.

Near Buckfastleigh we left the major roads and began traversing the smaller B roads. The lowland fields now gave way to high moorland and jagged promontories known locally as tors. At Princetown we made a small detour to the derelict Whiteworks tin mine. Covington

27

parked the car and Holmes and I got out and surveyed the vast bowl-shaped depression that lay before us. I saw a Dartmoor pony and watched with fascination as it moved between the tufts of cotton grass and shook the ground beneath its feet. Here was the remote expanse of peat bogs called Fox Tor Mires that inspired 'the Great Grimpen Mire' within 'the Supreme Adventure'. Holmes maintained his silence but I sensed him tighten in awe at the spectacle.

After returning to the car we backtracked to Princetown. Ten minutes later, Covington pulled-up behind an inn called 'The Plume of Feathers', which was built in 1785 and is the oldest building in the town. It is situated directly opposite the former 'Duchy Hotel' where Sir Arthur and Fletcher Robinson stayed in 1901 during a research trip to Dartmoor.

Soon we were ensconced in our room with our bags. Covington said good night and then retired to his own room for we had retained his services for the week. I peered out the window and saw the cold granite façade of Princetown Prison, the former home of Selden, the Notting Hill murderer.

"Well are these new quarters suitable?" asked Holmes breaking his silence for the first time since we departed London.

"I should say so Holmes! Shall we enquire after some dinner?"

"Good old Watson. You will never change!" laughed Holmes. He was clutching a small black rectangular instrument that was encrusted with buttons. Without warning a large cube mounted to the wall burst into life with sound and moving pictures. "TV Watson! Let's watch the news before we eat."

For the next hour, we sat on the edge of my bed and listened to a presenter deliver a monologue about the days' events, which was interspersed with related film. The program addressed local, national and international items that sounded much like what could have been told of in our day. From time to time the delivery of the news was interrupted by commercial advertisements that hawked everything from miraculous curatives for male ailments to hygiene products for women! Frankly I was unimpressed by this contraption. I saw promise in its usage but the reality of the program contents did not engage my interest. However, Holmes was clearly enthralled. As we left our room to go to dinner he mumbled, "What an age, what wonders?"

After concluding our dinner we shared a carafe of port. Holmes was in a contemplative mood and spent much of his time observing our fellow diners. He said little and nor did I. We were both feeling tired.

On retiring, Holmes bade me good night, and I retreated to the bathroom to investigate the modern miracles that had been wrought in plumbing. Of course showers had existed in our day but they were nothing like this one, which produced torrents of hot water for so long as I desired. What luxury!

Chapter VII

Independent enquiries

Next morning, I awoke to the ringing of the telephone. I reached over for the noisy contrivance and managed a sleepy, "Hello, Watson here."

"Good morning Dr. Watson." came a cheery, youthful female voice. "This is your wake-up call."

"What? My dear, I do not recall requesting such a call!"

"Oh, well it must have been your friend then, Mr. Holmes. In any event, a man came to reception late last night and said that I should call at 6.30am. He also said that you must go to Fox Tor Café at 7.00am."

"Oh, I see. Well, thank you and good day." I replaced the receiver and stared sleepily at the ceiling. Confound the man I thought irritably!

Twenty minutes later I entered the café and located

Holmes drinking coffee at a table. "This really is quite good Watson." he said. "I hazard that it is not Turkish but nevertheless it is most flavoursome!"

"Well, I am glad that it meets your approval! Why did you wake me at this ungodly hour?" I complained.

"Watson I have a plan and I anticipate some action!"

"You have a plan?" I yawned hungrily.

"Indeed. I spent much of the night surfing on a laptop."

"You did what?" I started.

Holmes ignored my question and he continued, "It's an ingenious device! It has all the features of its larger desktop cousin but is infinitely more portable. Anyway, I did some so-called googling, and I discovered much useful information!"

"What did you discover?" I asked in bemusement.

Holmes beckoned to the waitress to bring him another coffee before he replied, "Roger la Pelure d'Ail is no literary man. In fact, he is a former undertaker, property developer and driving instructor! Moreover he began his investigation into the links between Sir Arthur and Fletcher Robinson after he moved into the latter man's former home. So what do you make of it all Watson?"

"Well, it sounds to me that la Pelure d'Ail is seeking to cash in on the history of his home," said I.

"Quite!" agreed Holmes.

"So what do you propose we do about it?" I asked.

"After breakfast, I want you to visit Princetown Library and use a computer to unearth what you can about the relationship between Sir Arthur and Fletcher Robinson."

"Holmes, I lack your computer skills but I wager they still have books and files. And I am sure that the staff will help me to use a machine. What are you going to do?" I queried.

"I want to do a little exploring of my own. I might also test my old talent for disguise! Let's meet back at the inn for dinner at say 8pm?"

"Okay." I consented.

Holmes got to his feet and left to find Covington and the car. I settled the bill and then strolled to Two Bridges to kill some time before the library opened. At 10.00am I entered Princetown Library and spent the rest of the morning doing research. Within three hours, thanks to the assistance of one Miss Janeway, I too was proficient in the basic use of a computer.

At 1.00pm the library closed for an hour, so I went to the 'Old Police Station' for a fish and chip lunch. However, the fast-food was not to my taste and I endured a little dyspeptic discomfort for a while afterwards. Shortly after 2.00pm I returned to the library and continued my efforts till 5.00pm when it shut. Having bid a good evening to my new friend, Miss Janeway, I returned to the inn to await Holmes' arrival. I felt sure that he would be delighted by my findings.

At 8.00pm, I entered the dining room and was surprised to see that Holmes was absent. I waited for about an hour before finally ordering an appetiser of brie and crackers. Whilst eating, I spied a tall thin man with a bald pate, yellow teeth and dirty overalls approaching my table. He paused in front of me and smiled broadly.

"Couldn't wait for me, eh?"

"Holmes!" I exclaimed in astonishment.

"My dear Watson, you are too readily deceived!"

Chapter VIII

Roger la Pelure d'Ail

Holmes studied the menu intensely. "Watson, please order for me a rare sirloin steak with vegetables and I will rejoin you shortly." After he left, I called the waitress, and placed an order for two rare steaks and a bottle of Cabernet. Ten minutes later Holmes returned in a more customary guise.

"I'm famished Watson! How did you do today?"

As Holmes spoke our food arrived and he said no more. Instead, he tore into his meal, and drained a glass of wine. I took the cue and began to relate my findings to him:

"Well, I made good progress. I visited the library, and with the aid of a charming assistant, I managed to use the computer there. I discovered that modern crime investigation has made giant leaps. It seems that a post mortem can now reveal whether Fletcher Robinson died of poisoning, typhoid, or some other cause.

"Very good Watson but I am afraid that this information will be totally useless to us in our endeavour."

"Why?" I demanded.

"Detective Inspector Moore has just informed me by telephone that the Home Office will not permit the exhumation of Fletcher Robinson." replied Holmes.

"Why?" I persisted.

"Because the persons that allegedly conspired to kill him are themselves deceased and can't stand trial!"

"So how can we rebut the accusations that have been levelled against Sir Arthur?" I complained.

"Apparently there are now forensic tests that will detect the presence of laudanum in keratin. Hence, if we can obtain some hair or nail that was growing on Fletcher

Robinson at around the time of his death, we might be able to discredit the murder allegation.

"And just how do we do that?" I asked incredulously.

"There may be a way but it's a long story Watson!"

"Please reveal all!" I implored.

"I paid a visit to Mr. Roger la Pelure d'Ail. It was most illuminating" replied Holmes. After a brief pause for dramatic effect he continued: "It was all quite easy. I simply knocked on his door and pretended to be a cable TV repair man. Mr. la Pelure d'Ail answered my call and told me that his TV set was functioning properly. I replied that we had received reports of disruption to signals in the area and that I had been assigned to check all local connections. He appeared to accept my story."

"But Holmes you don't know anything about cable TV do you?"

"No, but I obtained the use of a uniform and a van from Covington's brother who lives near Ipplepen. He is a genuine cable TV man, and he filled me in, for a small consideration of course."

"You drove the van!" I exclaimed in horror.

"No, Covington did. He then returned to his brother's house and waited for me to conclude my business."

"What did you learn?" I asked impatiently.

"Well, la Pelure d'Ail is a rather garrulous individual. He is about sixty years old and wears a tweed shooting jacket which makes him look like a country squire. He does not own the former Fletcher Robinson residence, which I now know to be called Park Hill House. The property has been converted into six flats and he merely rents one of them!"

"...and?" I interjected expectantly.

"...and la Pelure d'Ail showed me the TV in his living room. I squeezed myself behind the set and checked all the connections. I took my time about it and made a real show using a marvellous gadget that tests whether a circuit is live. I also engaged la Pelure d'Ail in a conversation and asked how long he had lived at Park Hill House. He replied that he had moved there twelve years ago."

"What else did he say?" I urged.

Holmes continued, "Then I casually enquired after the history of the house. He became very animated and told me that the house had once belonged to man called Bertram Fletcher Robinson, a close friend of the famous writer, Sir Arthur Conan Doyle. Ironically, he asked me whether I had read *The Hound of the Baskervilles*! No said I."

"What did he say to that Holmes?"

"He said that Fletcher Robinson had entertained Conan Doyle in this very room many times and that the rest was history as they say!"

Chapter IX
Chasing down the quarry

After dinner, we retreated to the bar and I ordered two cognacs. I was just beginning to ponder how the days' events might permit us to advance our cause when Holmes suddenly said, "I told la Pelure d'Ail that I would need to revisit him tomorrow with an updated cable connector and he was amenable to the suggestion. I then noticed that his eyes were glazed and his breath smelt of whisky. Evidently the man enjoys a drink. So I told him that I was fascinated by the history of his house - that I would schedule him in for my last stop tomorrow - and that I would give him a bottle of Glenlivet if he would show me around the place. He willingly agreed. Previous to all of this, I had observed an Edwardian silver locket atop the mantelpiece by the television set. Do you suppose that it might contain strands of Fletcher Robinson's hair?"

"Holmes, now I see! If that locket contains Fletcher Robinson's hair then we can test it for laudanum!"

"That is most perspicacious of you my dear Watson! I also noticed a few other items on a small writing desk that might shed further light on Roger la Pelure d'Ail's scheme. For example, he had several magazines about dog husbandry. They each related to a single breed."

"Which breed?" I asked excitedly.

"The Bull Mastiff!" replied Holmes.

"Good grief Holmes! What kind of fiendish plot is this man hatching?"

"I am not entirely sure but no doubt he has something spectacular in mind." Holmes remarked enigmatically.

"What does he hope to gain by all this?"

Holmes did not answer me immediately. Instead he ordered a second cognac and considered my question thoughtfully. Eventually he said, "I believe the answer to be most elementary. The man is a publicity seeker. He has produced a book and hopes that his actions will help to sell it. Mr. la Pelure d'Ail is motivated by greed Watson."

"But to what ends would he use such a fearsome dog?" I persisted.

"I believe he wishes to set it loose periodically in order to scare the locals and revive the old stories of spectral hounds. Such actions would draw attention to his book and further his game!"

"That makes a good deal of sense Holmes but how do we expose him?"

"I intend to cultivate a friendship with la Pelure d'Ail. Then, after I have secured his trust, I will lavish him with liberal quantities of whisky to loosen his tongue. Finally, I may use another marvel of modern technology called a Dictaphone to record a confession. That should do for him!"

Chapter X

A gigantic hound

At 11.00am the next day, Holmes left with Covington to begin his preparations for entrapping la Pelure d'Ail. Left to my own devices, I decided to take a stroll to the stunted oak trees at Wistman's Wood near Two Bridges. I returned to the inn during the early afternoon, and after a quick snack, I headed off to the library to undertake further research.

At 5.00pm the library closed and I bade a fond farewell to Miss Janeway for a second day in a row. I returned to my room at the inn and then read for a while. Around 7.30pm, I descended the stairs from our room to the dining room. After twenty minutes, I surrendered to my hunger and ordered a plate of corned beef and cabbage, and a carafe of white wine. On this occasion, Holmes arrived without disguise and just as I was preparing to order a dessert.

He offered no excuse for his late arrival. Neither did he

provide any explanation for his protracted absence. He merely caught the eye of the waitress, placed an order for steak and kidney pudding, and helped himself to my glass of wine.

"How did you progress?" I asked cautiously. Holmes stared at me with steeled-eyes before replying, "Most significantly!" I began to feel alarmed by his manner and asked, "Whatever is wrong?"

"Roger la Pelure d'Ail is about to commit a very foolish act Watson! He may endanger not only himself but quite possibly many innocent people, and all for some foolish notion that he might make a name for himself, and some quick money too."

"Go on!" I implored him.

"As you know I paid him a visit late this afternoon. I produced a bottle of Glenlivet and he drank nearly half the bottle! He then showed me around the grounds of Park Hill House in an electrically powered vehicle that he called a golf cart. After some five minutes had elapsed, we happened upon an outbuilding that was fortified with a barbed wire fence and barred windows. My host tried to steer us away from it but I had sufficient time to observe a most disturbing sight upon the ground."

"For heavens sake Holmes, what did you see?"

"Watson, I saw the footprints of a gigantic hound!"

Holmes continued, "My host began to display the effects of intoxication and his resentment came bubbling up. He told me that the local people do not like him and that they treat him as an interloper! He vowed to square matters with them very soon!"

"What was your response to that Holmes?"

"Of course I clucked sympathetically from time to time. I also added that I too found the local residents to be cold. My response appeared to please him because he dozed off in the chair. I then ran the short distance back to his flat and recovered the silver locket from the mantelpiece in his living room. I opened it carefully and saw to my satisfaction that it contained both hair and a photograph of Fletcher Robinson. Using sterile forceps I removed a sample of the hair and placed it in a small forensic jiffy bag that was posted to me by Detective Inspector Moore. Look, I have it here!"

"But how can we know when the hair was clipped? It might predate the period when Fletcher Robinson was allegedly poisoned." I reasoned.

"Of course that is a possibility Watson. However, the locket bears an inscription to Mrs. Fletcher Robinson, and it is dated Christmas '06. That is less than a month before Fletcher Robinson died. I fear that is as good as we can get."

"But Holmes, why do you continue to look so worried?

Holmes sat perfectly still and looked at me with a

penetrating stare. "Watson, after recovering the hair, I returned to la Pelure d'Ail and sped his revival with smelling salts. Once awake he continued in the same vein of self-indignation that he had displayed before losing consciousness. He told me that he would fix the local residents and literary types. He added that he would start tomorrow night and that I should be sure to watch the TV news over the forthcoming days! He then slumped into his chair and succumbed to his stupor."

"What action did you take next?" I spluttered.

"I made my way to the rear of the outbuilding and found a gap in the wall that enabled me to see inside. I peered through and beheld a huge coal-black Bull Mastiff. It was foaming at the mouth and pulling with the force of several men at a tether that was secured to the floor by two iron hooks!"

"So what's our next move?" I hesitated.

"Tomorrow morning we will send the hair sample to

Scotland Yard. I have already liaised with Detective Inspector Moore over the telephone and he assures me that the forensic laboratory will complete the necessary tests just as soon as they possibly can. We must also keep la Pelure d'Ail under close surveillance in order to prevent him from committing some heinous act with his diabolical hound!"

Chapter XI

A near escape

Next morning Covington drove Holmes to Plymouth Central Police Station where he had arranged to meet a courier who could transport the precious hair sample to New Scotland Yard. I once again returned to the library to examine some potentially useful items that I had turned up during my visit there the previous day. As usual Miss Janeway was on-hand to both welcome and assist me.

Amongst the many papers that I read were several that had been published by The Sherlock Holmes Society of London. Several of these refuted the claims that had been made by la Pelure d'Ail. For example one read, 'The whole matter is bunkum! These allegations are a complete fabrication. Undoubtedly, Fletcher Robinson was the origin for the idea that inspired *The Hound of the Baskervilles*, however the narrative for the tale was written by Conan Doyle alone!'

It was most gratifying to view the strength of feeling which existed within the three hundred such societies that persisted throughout the world at that time. I was flattered to learn that the stories of our adventures are still so widely read and I began to feel a little nostalgic!

Around midday, I returned to the inn for a prearranged luncheon engagement with Holmes. Buoyed by my findings that morning, I greeted my partner with a broad smile, which he totally ignored.

"Watson! I wager that we will have action shortly! Did you bring your old service revolver?"

"Yes I did, although I never imagined that we would use it!" I replied uncertainly.

"Just a precautionary measure I assure you dear chap. I don't fear Roger la Pelure d'Ail as such but I do fear his judgment, or lack of it. I worry that he may unleash a force of nature that he is unable to control!"

"So what should we do now?" I mused.

"I think that we must go to Ipplepen and watch for what might develop."

After a light lunch we sped away in the car. Covington dropped us off about two hundred yards to the west of Ipplepen. Fifteen minutes later, we were lying under a holly bush, which overlooked a pathway that meandered towards Park Hill House.

Many hours passed. We lay in silence as a full moon rose and shed its light upon the eerie estate. Whisps of mist clustered about the bases of the nearby trees. I felt uncomfortable and my legs began to stiffen. I slowly stretched them out and then rubbed the muscles to keep my circulation up. Suddenly an owl flapped its way out of a nearby tree and startled the pair of us.

"What time is it?" whispered Holmes.

"It is 10.25pm!" I whispered back.

"Watson if nothing happens by midnight, I think that we should call it a night!"

"Good!" I consented.

Then we heard it! At first it was nothing more than a distant moan. But it soon drew closer and gained in intensity. There could be no mistaking that noise. It was the blood-curdling howl of a furious hound!

"Watson!"

"Yes!" I gasped.

"I think it is coming from over there. Let's go and see."

We broke cover and dashed forth, keeping so far as was possible, to the shadows produced by the moonlit trees. Again we heard the howl and the hairs upon the nape of my neck stood upright! Quickly, we located the main pathway and briefly paused to fix the direction of the noise. Another howl pounded my eardrums. It was almost upon us this time.

"Stop! Stop! Get back I say!" I heard a man shriek.

"Roger la Pelure d'Ail!" cried Holmes.

The cacophony of noises was now deafening. I drew my service revolver and dashed towards the commotion. Headlong I rushed until I came upon a man bursting out of the mist. His whitened face was contorted with fear. A few yards behind him, I beheld a gigantic hell-hound with drool slathering from its muzzle.

"No. No! I'm your master! Stop. Stop!" grimaced la Pelure d'Ail.

His protestations ended abruptly as the hound leapt on his back and drove him to the ground with a resounding thud. The man crumpled like a child's doll. He briefly raised his right arm in a futile gesture of self protection. However, the hound simply seized upon it and shook it, as if it were a twig.

"Shoot Watson! Shoot!" yelled Holmes.

Without hesitation I took aim and unloaded two rounds. It appeared that I had hit my target because the hound momentarily shuddered and released its grip. It then turned its gaze on me and bolted in my direction. I fired off two more rounds as the beast sprang at my throat. It continued to sail through the air before it crashed into me and sent me sprawling to the ground. For a moment I lay dazed beside the lifeless body of the beast.

"Watson! That was excellent marksmanship. You still have your military streak running deep!" said Holmes as he raised me to my feet and dusted me off.

"Good Lord Holmes! That was far too close!" I blurted after imbibing several sips of medicinal brandy from my hip flask. "Is the man alive?" I asked.

"Yes. But he is in deep shock. Let's get him inside so you can examine him more thoroughly."

We lifted la Pelure d'Ail, and supporting his weight between us, we trudged along the path towards Park Hill House. Half-way there Holmes called a halt and said, "Let's stop for a minute. We could use a breather and I need to make a quick telephone call."

We set our charge down on a tree stump. He was semi-conscious and mumbling incomprehensibly to himself. Holmes produced a mobile phone from his jacket pocket and punched away at the buttons.

"Inspector?... It's Holmes here. Have you arrived yet?... Good! We have la Pelure d'Ail but he requires urgent medical attention. Can you meet us at Park Hill House within the hour?... Perfect!"

Holmes returned the phone to his pocket. He then said with discernible sympathy, "Come Watson, let's get this wretched creature back to the house."

Chapter XII

Striking a deal

With much effort we finally managed to half-carry, and half-drag, la Pelure d'Ail back to Park Hill House. We entered the house through a door that led to a communal games room. Carefully we laid our patient down on a threadbare couch. I located a blanket that was draped over a recliner and used it to cover him.

Gradually la Pelure d'Ail began to recover his senses. He was shocked and had some superficial cuts to his right arm but he was otherwise uninjured. After twenty minutes, he regained full consciousness and opened his eyes warily.

"What happened? How did I get here? Who are you people?" he clamoured.

"Please don't be alarmed. My name is Sherlock Holmes and this is my associate, Dr. Watson."

The man's eyes widened and he hissed, "How can that be? You're not real!"

"I assure you Mr. la Pelure d'Ail that we are very real" asserted Holmes.

I added, "We are real because many people believe in us. Your actions and plans might have jeopardised our continued existence!"

Roger la Pelure d'Ail made a feeble attempt to rise. I stopped him. "There sir! Lay still and you will soon begin to feel better." He lowered his head and a look of resignation spread across his face.

Holmes said, "We discerned your plan. Your idea was

to use your hound to generate publicity in order to sell your new book. Oh yes, we know everything!" He then offered la Pelure d'Ail a glass of Glenlivet. "You like this brand I gather?" The man narrowed his eyes and spluttered, "You're the cable TV repair man!"

"Quite!" replied Holmes. "Now listen to me carefully! The authorities are on their way and they will arrive here shortly. So far as I can see you have yet to commit any crime. We will testify that your dog was a pet and that it got loose and attacked you. However in return, you must retract the allegations that you directed against Sir Arthur Conan Doyle and instruct your publisher to withdraw your book from sale. Furthermore, you must agree to live out the rest of your retirement peaceably."

Roger la Pelure d'Ail said nothing at first. He simply turned his head towards the window and stared into the distance. Finally, he returned his guilty gaze to Holmes and whispered, "I don't know what is going on here but I do know when it's time to fold 'em. I'll do as you say Mr. Holmes. I can see that I've bitten off far more than

I can chew!"

Before Holmes had time to respond the door to the games room was flung open and in bundled Detective Inspector Moore. Holmes acknowledged the man with a slight tilt of his head and a pursed smile.

"Holmes, Watson! The ambulance will be here shortly. Tell me what has happened!"

Holmes shot a quick glance at Roger la Pelure d'Ail and without equivocation he stated, "This man was attacked by his guard dog. It got loose and then mauled him. Beyond that there is nothing to tell."

Moore stood motionless. He appeared to be evaluating his options. After several seconds, and much to the visible relief of la Pelure d'Ail, he simply remarked, "Very well Mr. Holmes, so long as you are sure?" It was clear to me that Moore and Holmes had forged some prior agreement.

Shortly after midnight la Pelure d'Ail was wheeled out to an awaiting ambulance. Just before he was hoisted into the back of this remarkable machine he softly said, "Holmes, Watson. Thank you. You saved my life! I have been a dreadful fool and I am sorry. Please don't worry about me. You may rely upon my word!"

Holmes nodded his head approvingly and responded, "I know Mr. la Pelure d'Ail. Good luck to you sir and I hope that you enjoy a long and relaxed retirement."

After the ambulance had left, Detective Inspector Moore rejoined us and asked Holmes what really happened.

"Let us just say that his literary career is now over. I don't see that la Pelure d'Ail has committed any crime beyond the possible mistreatment of a dog. However, I think you will agree with me that this is a moot point?"

"Holmes, I do and as I told you earlier over the phone our forensic tests have revealed no sign of poison of any kind in the hair sample that you provided!"

"Holmes! You knew about the hair?" I exclaimed.

"Indeed I did Watson. Once I had that information, I knew that Roger la Pelure d'Ail was a fraud and that we had him in check-mate. If he had refused my bargain, I would have leaked the results of the forensic test to the press, and silenced him that way instead!"

"Mr. Holmes, Dr. Watson, it has been a great honour to work with you both and I shall never forget it. Is there any other way in which I may be of assistance to you?"

Holmes looked thoughtful for a moment. "Well, there is one thing Inspector Moore. Do you think that you could arrange for us to fly to London from Exeter Airport?"

"I will see what can be done Mr. Holmes!" he replied, and we all laughed.

Chapter XIII

Precautionary notes

Two days later, Covington collected us from Heathrow Airport. On our arrival at Baker Street, Holmes insisted that I undertake one last task, and compile the evidence that I had collated at Princetown Library, which refuted the claims that had been made by Roger la Pelure d'Ail. Holmes reasoned that this might deter other would-be conspirators. This I was happy to do and a synopsis of my findings is reproduced on the following pages. After I completed this final request, Holmes, Mrs. Hudson, Wiggins and I all bade a fond farewell to each other and we retreated to the pages of books that were written long ago – our reputations still very much intact!

The following abbreviations denote:

BFR = Bertram Fletcher Robinson
ACD = Arthur Conan Doyle

21 May 1901. BFR had an article published in the *Daily Express* entitled *'Truthful Jean' on the War – The Yarns of M. Jean Carrere, the only French War Correspondent with our Army in South Africa.* In this item, BFR reviewed an autobiographical account of the Boer War entitled *La Guerre Transvaal – En Pleine Epopée* ('The Transvaal War – At the Height of the Epic'). This book was written by Jean Carreres, a correspondent for a French newspaper called *Le Matin.* The book is generally critical of British foreign policy and attitudes, but it is complimentary about ACD, a point that is stressed by BFR in his article thus:

> "What a man!" cried the enthusiastic Frenchman; "and what a brave man! How his merciful and thoughtful words consoled me after the foolish rodomontades [pretentious boastings] I had listened to!" He ought to write a book on the war" - M. Carrere was gifted with a spirit of prophecy - "I do not know if in his style and in the impression his adventures left on him he will be better or worse than Kipling; but I am certain that he will be more humane - more impartial...He loves and defends the English soldier but he understands the spirit of the Boer and it is in that the secret of justice lies."

25 May 1901. The following promotional announcement was made in *Tit-Bits* before the publication of *The Hound of the Baskervilles.* This periodical was like *The Strand Magazine* also published by Sir George Newnes. Significantly, this announcement appeared before ACD and BFR had visited Dartmoor together (31 May-2 June 1901). This indicates that they had already come to some amicably agreement concerning the authorship of the story:

The Revival of Sherlock Holmes

**Very many readers of The Strand Magazine have asked
us over and over again if we could not induce Mr.
Conan Doyle to give us some more stories of this
wonderful character. Mr. Conan Doyle has been
engaged on other work, but presently he will give us an
important story to appear in the Strand, in which the
great Sherlock Holmes is the principle character. It will
appear in both the British and American editions. In
America the play founded upon the career of the great
detective has run for many months with enormous
success. It is going to be produced in London in about
three months, and at the same time the new Sherlock
Holmes story will commence in the Strand. It will be
published as a serial of from 30,000 to 50,000 words,
and the plot is one of the most interesting and striking
that have ever been put before us. We are sure that all
those readers of the Strand who have written to us on
the matter, and those who have not, will be very glad
that Mr. Conan Doyle is going to give us some more
about our old favourite.**

August 1901. The first of nine monthly instalments of *The Hound
of the Baskervilles* was published in the British edition of *The
Strand Magazine*. BFR's contribution was fully acknowledged in a
brief footnote that appeared on the first page of the first Chapter:

**This story owes its inception to my friend, Mr. Fletcher
Robinson, who has helped me both in the general plot
and in the local details. — A.C.D.**

[N.B. This serialisation was also published in the American edition
of *The Strand Magazine*. Each of the nine instalments trailed by
one month its counterpart in the British edition].

25 March 1902. *The Hound of the Baskervilles* was published as a
novel by George Newnes (London). This book preceded by one
month the conclusion of the serialised story in the British version of

The Strand Magazine. The English book edition includes a short, foreword-like epistolary on its own page which reads:

MY DEAR ROBINSON,

> *It was to your account of a West-*
> *Country legend that this tale owes its incep-*
> *tion. For this and for your help in the*
> *details all thanks.*
> *Yours most truly,*

> > *A. CONAN DOYLE.*
> > **HINDHEAD, HASLEMERE.**

Thereafter, BFR gave first edition copies of this book to The Rev. Robert Duins Cooke, Agnes Cooke (Robert's wife) and Henry 'Harry' Baskerville. During May 1901, The Rev. Robert Cooke had assisted BFR in mapping-out the fictional locations for *The Hound of the Baskervilles*. Later that same month, Baskerville drove BFR and ACD about Dartmoor during their research trip there. The following inscriptions, in BFR's hand-writing, concede to the extent of his involvement with the story:

> **To Rev. R D Cooke from the assistant plot producer,**
> **Bertram Fletcher Robinson**

> **To Mrs. Cooke, with the kind regards of the assistant**
> **plot producer, Bertram Fletcher Robinson**

> **To Harry Baskerville from B Fletcher Robinson with**
> **apologies for using the name!**

15 April 1902. *The Hound of the Baskervilles* was published as a novel by McClure, Phillips & Company (New York). This was the first American edition of the book, and it includes a version of ACD's acknowledgement letter to BFR:

MY DEAR ROBINSON

It was your account of a west country legend which first suggested the idea of this little tale to my mind.

For this, and for the help which you gave me in its evolution, all thanks. Yours most truly, A. Conan Doyle.

[N.B. This version was written from dictation on 26 January 1902 by Major Charles Terry (ACD's Secretary). It therefore predates the version that was published in the first English book edition].

31 October 1903. ACD had a Sherlock Holmes story entitled *The Adventure of the Norwood Builder* published in *Collier's Weekly Magazine*. In this story, an innocent person is incriminated for a murder by the use of a wax mould to falsify their thumbprint. Harold Michelmore (BFR's solicitor and school friend) recorded that ACD bought this idea from BFR during a voyage aboard a steamship called *Briton* in July 1900. It is improbable that ACD would have risked using this idea if there were any prevailing controversy over the authorship of *The Hound of the Baskervilles*.

January 1904. BFR, ACD & a mutual friend called Max Pemberton (later Sir Max) were each elected to a twelve-man London-based criminological group referred to by its members as 'Our Society'.

18 June 1904. Both BFR and ACD attended a dinner at the Savoy Hotel in London. This event was held in honour of Lord Roberts and was hosted by Joseph Hodges Choate (U.S. Ambassador to the United Kingdom). The guest list was restricted to members of an Anglo-American society called 'The Pilgrims'.

23 June 1904. ACD had a 'Letter to the Editor' published in *Vanity Fair* under the heading of *M.C.C. Absolutism*. BFR had recently replaced Oliver Armstrong Fry as the editor of this journal. ACD, a keen cricketer and himself a member of the Marlyebone Cricket Club, began his letter thus:

Sir,—You were good enough to ask me for my opinion of the management of the M.C.C.

Clearly, BFR had relied upon his friendship with ACD to persuade the latter to write on the topic (probably during the dinner they both attended on 18 June 1904). This suggests that there was no friction between BFR and ACD over the authorship of *The Hound of the Baskervilles*.

7 July 1904. BFR had an article entitled *On Political Lies – A Growing Danger in British Politics*, published in *Vanity Fair*. In this item, BFR condemned the way in which some political parties (especially The Liberal Party and Labour Party) were increasingly using misinformation to support their causes. He cites lies being told about the Second Boer War, exaggerations about rising food prices and the falsification of data pertaining to the number of Chinese immigrants working the mines. He exemplified the situation with a case involving his friend, ACD:

> **In the last General Election, Sir Arthur Conan Doyle was standing for a division of Edinburgh. The honesty of his convictions and his hard hitting, straight-forward oratory won him the hearts even of political opponents. He had made great progress in the centre of a Radical stronghold, and his election seemed certain. On the day of the poll, however, the constituency was placarded with posters, stating in four-feet letters that Conan Doyle was a Roman Catholic, and that the Church of Scotland was in danger.**

> **This Radical lie – for Sir Arthur does not happen to be a Roman catholic – caused the desired consternation. The worthy Scotsmen read, exclaimed in horror, and hurried to the polls to avert this terrible danger. An honourable method of winning an election surely!**

Following publication of the preceding article, several supportive 'Letters to the Editor' were sent to *Vanity Fair*. BFR's reference to the integrity of ACD is particularly relevant given that it was

70

written more than two years after the publication of *The Hound of the Baskervilles.* Evidently BFR still held ACD in high esteem and was satisfied with the outcome of their literary collaboration during 1901.

August 1904. BFR had the first in a series of six detective short stories collectively entitled *The Chronicles of Addington Peace,* published in the *Lady's Home Magazine of Fiction.* The first instalment was by-lined as follows:

Joint author with Sir Arthur Conan Doyle in his Best Sherlock Holmes Story The Hound of the Baskervilles.

There is no indication that ACD ever objected to this statement. Hence it appears that he was willing to allow his name to be used to market BFR's work (see December 1905, 1906 & 5 November-14 December 1906).

22 November 1904. *The Times* newspaper reported the publication of Sir John Robinson's autobiography entitled *Fifty Years on Fleet Street* (McMillan & Company Limited of London). This book includes the following statement that was made in the Foreword, which was written by Frederick Moy Thomas, a former employee of Sir John's (BFR's uncle) for over twenty-five years:

I am much indebted to Sir Arthur Conan Doyle for leave to publish his striking letter to Sir John Robinson on the subject of America and the Americans [dated 3rd November 1894]... and to a number of Sir John's relatives and friends for similar facilities or for valuable counsel or assistance.

Clearly ACD had granted permission for his letter to be reproduced in Sir John's autobiography. This implies that ACD and the Robinson family were still on friendly terms some three years after the publication of *The Hound of the Baskervilles.*

1905. BFR had eight short detective stories published in a book entitled *The Chronicles of Addington Peace* (Harper & Brother,

London). Undoubtedly, this development was due in part to ACD's willingness to allow his name to be associated with these stories (see August 1904). Later, BFR's book was listed in *Queens Quorum: A History of the Detective-Crime Short Story as Revealed by the 106 Most Important Books Published in this Field Since 1845*.

July 1905. BFR was invited to contribute an item entitled *My Best Story* to *The Novel Magazine*. This periodical was owned by Cyril Arthur Pearson and it was edited by Percy Everett. Both BFR and Everett were employed by Pearson to work as journalists for the *Daily Express* newspaper between 1900 and 1904. Furthermore, BFR was the Godfather of Everett's daughter, Geraldine Winn Everett (6 February 1903 - 21 January 1998). In the preamble to the featured story, *The Debt of Heinrich Hermann*, BFR wrote:

> **Sir Arthur Conan Doyle is a type of the strong, clear-headed, generous Englishman, a very contrast to all that appertains to decadence. Yet there are many horrors in 'Sherlock Holmes'. It was from assisting him in 'The Hound of the Baskervilles' that I obtained my first lesson in the art of story construction. Imagination without that art is poor enough.**

This quote is important for several reasons. Firstly, it is the only quote about ACD and *The Hound of the Baskervilles* that is directly attributable to BFR. Secondly, it shows that BFR continued to hold ACD in high esteem some four years after the publication of the first episode of the story in the British edition of *The Strand Magazine* (August 1901). Finally, it reveals that it was ACD who devised the story as it appeared in the various first editions of the final narrative.

26 November 1905. A reporter called H. J. W. Dam had an article published in the *Sunday Magazine* supplement of *The New York Tribune*. This article is entitled *Arthur Conan Doyle – An Appreciation of the Author of 'Sir Nigel', the Great Romance Which Begins Next Sunday*. It includes an account of BFR's recollections about his trip to Dartmoor with ACD during 1901. There is no

evidence that BFR harbored any residual ill-feeling towards ACD within the following quote:

One of the most interesting weeks that I have ever spent was with Doyle on Dartmoor. He made the journey in my company shortly after I told him, and he had accepted from me, a plot which eventuated in the 'Hound of the Baskervilles'. Dartmoor, the great wilderness of bog and rock that cuts Devonshire at this point, appealed to his imagination. He listened eagerly to my stories of ghost hounds, of the headless riders and of the devils that lurk in the hollows – legends upon which I have been reared, for my home lay on the boarders of the moor. How well he turned to account his impressions will be remembered by all readers of 'The Hound'.

Two incidents come especially to my recollection. In the centre of the moor lies the famous convict prison of Princetown. In the great granite buildings, swept by the rains and clouded in the mists, are lodged over a thousand criminals, convicted on the more serious offences. A tiny village clusters at the foot of the slope on which they stand, and a comfortable old-fashioned inn affords accommodation to travellers.

The morning after our arrival Doyle and I were sitting in the smoking-room when a cherry-cheeked maid opened the door and announced 'Visitors to see you, gentlemen'. In marched four men, who solemnly sat down and began to talk about the weather, the fishing in the moor streams and other general subjects. Who they might be I had not the slightest idea. As they left I followed them into the hall of the inn. On the table were their four cards. The governor of the prison, the deputy governor, the chaplain and the doctor had come, as a pencil note explained, 'to call on Mr. Sherlock Holmes.'

One morning I took Doyle to see the mighty bog, a thousand acres of quaking slime, at any part of which a horse and rider might disappear, which figured so prominently in The Hound. He was amused at the story I told him of the moor man who on one occasion saw a hat near the edge of the morass and poked at it with a long pole he carried. 'You leave my hat alone!' came a voice from beneath it. 'Whoi'! Be there a man under 'at?' cried the startled rustic. 'Yes, you fool, and a horse under the man.'

From the bog we tramped eastward to the stone fort of Grimspound, which the savages of the Stone Age in Britain, the aborigines who were earlier settlers than Saxons or Danes or Norsemen, raised with enormous labour to act as a haven of refuge from marauding tribes to the South. The good preservation in which the Grimspound fort still remains is marvellous. The twenty-feet slabs of granite – how they were ever hauled to their places is a mystery to historian and engineer – still encircle the stone huts where the tribe lived. Into one of these Doyle and I walked, and sitting down on the stone which probably served the three thousand year-old chief as a bed we talked of the races of the past. It was one of the loneliest spots in Great Britain. No road came within a long distance of the place. Strange legends of lights and figures are told concerning it. Add thereto that it was a gloomy day overcast with heavy cloud.

Suddenly we heard a boot strike against a stone without and rose together. It was only a lonely tourist on a walking excursion, but at sight of our heads suddenly emerging from the hut he let out a yell and bolted. Our subsequent disappearance was due to the fact that we both sat down and rocked with laughter, and as he did not return I have small doubt Mr. Doyle and I added yet another proof of the supernatural to tellers of ghost stories concerning Dartmoor.

December 1905. An American newspaper, *The Detroit News* ran an eighteen part serialisation of BFR's 'Addington Peace' stories under the revised title of the *Inspector Grey Stories*. Each episode was by-lined as follows (see August 1904):

**By B. Fletcher Robinson,
Collaborator With SIR A. CONAN DOYLE.**

1906. P. F. Collier & Sons of New York published the first in a series of three anthologies entitled *Great Short Stories, Volume 1*

(1): Detective Stories (edited by William Patten). This book features twelve stories written by Broughton Brandenburg (one), Arthur Conan Doyle (two), Anna Katherine Green (one), Edgar Allen Poe (three) and Robert Louis Stevenson (four). The twelfth and final story is *The Vanished Millionaire* by BFR and it is preceded by the following introduction:

> **Fletcher Robinson is a London Journalist, the editor of "Vanity Fair," and author of a dozen detective stories in which are recorded the startling adventures of Mr. Addington Peace of Scotland Yard. He collaborated with Conan Doyle in "The Hound of the Baskervilles." When some of these stories appeared in the American magazines, for an unexplained reason (presumably editorial) the name of the hero was changed to Inspector Hartley.**

This statement is important for two reasons. Firstly, it reveals that ACD and BFR were content to allow their work to be published within the same anthology. This weakens any contention that the two men were in conflict over the authorship of *The Hound of the Baskervilles*. Secondly, ACD recorded no objection to the comment about BFR's involvement with his story. Hence yet again, it appears that he was willing to allow his name to be used to promote BFR's work (see August 1904).

18 October 1906. It appears that both BFR and ACD attended a meeting of 'Our Society' at the home of Max Pemberton. The host delivered a paper entitled *An Attempt to Blackmail Me*.

20 October 1906. BFR played a round of golf with ACD and three others at Hindhead in Surrey (no doubt this engagement was arranged on 18 October 1906). The meeting is recorded as an entry within the personal diary of ACD's brother called 'Innes' Doyle (later Brigadier-General Doyle).

5 November-14 December 1906. An American newspaper, the *Oelwein Daily Register* ran an eighteen part serialisation of BFR's 'Addington Peace' stories under the revised title of the *Inspector*

Grey Stories. Each episode was by-lined as follows (see August 1904):

By B. Fletcher Robinson,
Collaborator With SIR A. CONAN DOYLE.

24 January 1907. The following messages accompanied two floral tributes that were sent to BFR's funeral service:

In loving memory of an old and valued friend from Arthur Conan Doyle

From 'Our Society,' with deepest regrets from fellow members

(These fellow members included both ACD and Max Pemberton).

May 1907. Shortly before his death, BFR was commissioned to write an article entitled *People Much Talked About in London* for the American edition of *Munsey's Magazine* (Vol. XXXVII, No. II). In his article, BFR wrote the following compliments in relation to ACD:

> **In Pall Mall, too, it is likely that we shall meet some of the more famous of English literary men bound for that most exclusive of clubs — the Athenaeum. Here comes that kindly giant, Sir Arthur Conan Doyle, the creator of Sherlock Holmes, prince of detectives. He is of a fine British type, a clear-headed, sport-loving, big-hearted patriot.**
>
> **A mention of the Athenaeum Club reminds me of a story Sir Arthur told me of his first visit, after election, [8th March 1901], to that home of the respectabilities. He walked up to the hall-porter and, desiring to introduce himself to that important person's notice, asked if there were any letters for Conan Doyle. Now the Athenaeum is a favorite resort of the clerical dignitaries, and the hall-porter, who had small**

acquaintance with literature, replied 'No, canon, there are no letters for you.'

Sir Arthur did not care to explain, and for some weeks he suffered much from the disapproving eye of the hall-porter. The suit of tweeds affected by the great novelist shocked that functionary deeply, and when one day Sir Arthur appeared in a long racing-coat, the spectacle had such an effect upon him that Doyle had to rush to the desk and explain that he was not a dignitary of the church, but a writer of tales to whom some latitude in dress might be allowed.

Sir Arthur is an earnest supporter of the rifle-club movement. He has erected targets for a miniature rifle-range at his house on the moors at Hindhead [founded in late 1900]. There you may observe groom and carpenter, mason and village blacksmith competing against one another on a Saturday afternoon in the same fashion as their forebears did with 'The Long' bow, winning Creçy and Agincourt thereby. Among them the novelist may be seen at his best, shooting with them, cheering them on with kindly words or awarding prizes, chiefly out of his own pocket.

1908. Max Pemberton had a story entitled *The Wheels of Anarchy* published by Cassell & Company Limited (London). This book includes the following Author's Note that appeared on a separate page that precedes the list of contents:

This story was suggested to me by the late B. Fletcher Robinson, a dear friend, deeply mourned. The subject was one in which he had interested himself for some years; and almost the last message I had from him expressed the desire that I would keep my promise and treat of the idea in a book. This I have now done, adding something of my own to the brief notes he left me, but chiefly bringing to the task an enduring gratitude for a friendship which nothing can replace.

The above statement suggests that BFR knew that he was dying and thereby refutes the allegation that his death was due to an acute and unnatural cause.

1912. ACD wrote a book entitled *The Lost World* that is narrated by a character called Edward E. Malone. There are many parallels between Malone and BFR. For example, both spent part of their 'boyhood' in the West Country, fished and exceeded six feet in height. Furthermore they each became accomplished rugby players, London-based journalists and loved a woman called Gladys. Hence it appears that ACD modelled Malone on BFR.

June 1929. ACD wrote the following comments in a preface to a collection of four Sherlock Holmes novellas entitled *The Complete Sherlock Holmes Long Stories* (London: John Murray):

Then came The Hound of the Baskervilles. It arose from a remark by that fine fellow, whose premature death was a loss to the world, Fletcher Robinson, that there was a spectral dog near his home on Dartmoor. That remark was the inception of the book, but I should add that the plot and every word of the actual narrative are my own.

[This book was published on 14 September 1929].

Available from MX Publishing Limited

Close to Holmes

A Look at the Connections between
Historical London, Sherlock Holmes and
Sir Arthur Conan Doyle.

Eliminate the Impossible

An Examination of the World of
Sherlock Holmes on Page and Screen.

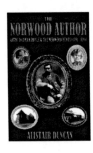

The Norwood Author

Arthur Conan Doyle and the
Norwood Years (1891 - 1894).

Available from MX Publishing Limited

In Search of Dr Watson

A Sherlockian Investigation.

[Fiction]

Arthur Conan Doyle, Sherlock Holmes and Devon

A Complete Tour Guide & Companion.

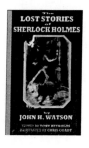

The Lost Stories of Sherlock Holmes

By Dr. John Watson M.D.

[Fiction]

www.mxpublishing.com

Available from MX Publishing Limited

Watson's Afghan Adventure

How Sherlock Holmes' Dr. Watson
became an Army Doctor.

[Fiction]

Shadowfall

A Novel of Sherlock Holmes.

[Fiction]

The Official Papers into the Matter Known as The Hound of the Baskervilles.

[Fiction]

www.mxpublishing.com

82

Available from MX Publishing Limited

Aside Arthur Conan Doyle

Twenty Original Tales by
Bertram Fletcher Robinson.

[Fiction]

Bertram Fletcher Robinson

A Footnote to
The Hound of the Baskervilles.

Wheels of Anarchy by Max Pemberton

As Recited from the Papers and the
Personal Narrative of his Secretary, Mr.
Bruce Ingersoll.

[Fiction]

www.mxpublishing.com

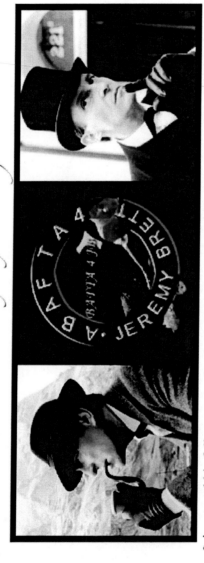
87

Lightning Source UK Ltd.
Milton Keynes UK
174026UK00006B/1/P